NEVER MIND!

DUKE THE DEAF DOG ASL SERIES

By Kelly Brakenhoff

Illustrated by Theresa Murray

*This publication was made possible in part by a grant
from the Sertoma Club of Omaha*

Copyright 2019 by Emerald Prairie Press

Photographs by Robert Chadwick of Robert Chadwick Photography

Published by Emerald Prairie Press

Cover Design and Interior Layout by Melissa Williams Design

Supplemental video content available on www.kellybrakenhoff.com

ISBN 978-1-7337424-1-2

*To my Deaf and hard of hearing friends.
I'm so grateful that you have filled my life with
laughter, your kindness,
and many hugs. ILY*

—Kelly

*To my husband for being so encouraging and to my
boys for their patience in helping this artist mom learn
new digital tricks.*

—Theresa

My friend and I were building a giant city with our toys.

My **friend** talked to me.
I didn't hear him.

friend

2

So I asked,
        "What did you say?"

My friend said,
    "Never mind."

6

One time at Sunday School my teacher told everyone to stand up and make a **line**. But I was coloring a picture and I didn't hear.

line

When I looked up everyone else was in line except me!

I said, "Sorry, I didn't know it was time to line up."

My teacher said,
    "Never mind."

My brothers and I were
playing tag at the park.

play

The other kids stared at me

and whispered.

12

They pointed at me and called
me a name.

I felt mad!

13

My brother said,
"Sometimes kids are just
mean. They don't know you
are cool."

We **walked** the other way and he said,
"Never mind them, let's go."

walk

During snack time at school all the kids and teachers talk at the same time.

I watch my friends **laughing**.

laughing

I watch my teacher helping my friend.

18

noisy

It's **noisy** and confusing and I don't know who is talking to me. It feels like a giant never mind.

Sometimes my mom
and dad talk to me.

Sometimes
they sign.

When we **eat** dinner,
everyone talks and signs.

eat

If I don't hear or see them, I ask, "What did you say?"

And my **mom** and **dad** tell me again.

Even if I have to ask twice!

mom

dad

My mom has a big rule.

She says, "In THIS house we don't say Never Mind!"

"Never Mind"
is not
allowed.

And I am so glad.

ASL Lesson

By Amy Willman, MS

The English words "never mind" can have different meanings in sentences, depending on the situation. However, American Sign Language (ASL) does not use a word-for-word translation of spoken English. In ASL, we don't use the signs for "never" and "mind" to represent that concept. ASL expresses different meanings by using facial expressions and hands. In this story, "never mind" has four different meanings, so we use four different ASL signs to express that idea.

Example 1)

English:	I didn't hear him, so I asked, "What did you say?". . . "Never mind."
ASL Sign:	"Nothing."
Meaning:	It's not important to say something again.

Example 2)

English:	When I looked up everyone else was in line except me. I said, "Sorry, I didn't know it was time to line up." . . ."Never mind."
ASL sign:	"Fine. Doesn't matter."
Meaning:	It's okay to go ahead and join them.

Example 3)

English:	My brother said, "Sometimes kids are just mean. They don't know you are cool." We walked the other way. . . "Never mind."
ASL sign:	"Don't worry." (Pppfff- use hand)
Meaning:	Those guys are rude, and we are better off without them.

Example 4)

English:	Its noisy and confusing and I don't know who is talking to me. . . . "Never mind."
ASL sign:	"Ignore me."
Meaning:	I feel like I am invisible in the room.

Example 5)

English:	My mom has a big rule: in this house. . . . "Never mind."
ASL sign:	"N-E-V-E-R M-I-N-D" (fingerspelling)
Meaning:	Fingerspelled words show strong impact in either positive or negative ways.

Bonus videos of Amy Willman demonstrating how to sign the ASL vocabulary words and story, and showing a Deaf parent signing the story in ASL are available on www.kellybrakenhoff.com

A Parent's Perspective | Chris Grassmeyer

My Deaf son might not even remember when I started our house rule. Max was 4 years old, and his older brother said "never mind" to him because Max didn't hear something. His face looked "deflated" to me, and I could see his self-value depleting. My heart hurt.

At dinner that evening I announced the rule, "Never mind is not allowed" in our home. When I explained why, Max's three older brothers seemed to understand that saying "never mind" made him feel un-important and excluded. I went on to say that he deserved to "hear" EVERYTHING that was being said to him. If our family took a little extra time to make sure Max understood what we said, he wouldn't feel left out.

I still heard "never mind" sometimes while my sons grew up, but all it took was "The Look" from Mom to the culprit and they tried again.

A Deaf Adult's Perspective | Max Grassmeyer

At home, I believe our house rule about not saying "never mind" helped my brothers understand my feelings because we were kids at the time. When I noticed it the most was especially in middle and high school when the hallways were as loud as a football stadium. No matter how hard I tried, I could not hear people well in that setting. Usually when I asked kids what they were talking about, they said, "Oh we're talking about something entirely different now," or "It's just stupid, whatever."

Living at home, I fit in a lot better, but now that I moved into the real world on my own, it happens everywhere I go. Even my coworkers talk while they work, and they switch conversation topics quickly. If I try to be involved, I can't work at the same time. I choose to focus on work because that's my job, so I don't mingle during work time.

Because I speak English fluently, it makes others confused. New people I meet never assume the fact I cannot hear things depending on background noises or if we aren't face to face while they talk to me. I have a cochlear implant, but I'm still Deaf and I use ASL. When my batteries die, or the technology breaks, I am Deaf. One of my favorite quotes says, "I'm as deaf as a tree can get." It can be frustrating to make people understand my situation.

The End

About the Contributors

Kelly Brakenhoff is an American Sign Language Interpreter whose motivation for learning ASL began in high school when she wanted to converse with her deaf friends. In her free time she's a half-marathon runner, chocolate lover, wife, mom and grandma, and Husker fan. She has published two mystery novels, *Death by Dissertation* and *Dead Week*. *Never Mind* is her first children's picture book. She and her husband have a 2 year old German Wirehair Pointer and an elderly Cockapoo. Follow her Facebook page @ kellybrakenhoffauthor for the latest news.

Theresa Murray has been creating custom art and murals for over 20 years. She pulls from her past as a grooming assistant to inspire the dog personalities for this series. Theresa lives in Omaha, Nebraska with her husband, two sons, and their Westie, Tinkerbell.

Amy Willman has worked as an American Sign Language Coordinator and Lecturer at the University of Nebraska-Lincoln since 2001. Before moving back to her childhood home in Nebraska, Amy taught elementary school for three years and taught ASL at Santa Fe Community College for six years. Her bachelor's degree in Elementary Level and Studio Arts is from Gallaudet University, the only Deaf university in the world. She earned her master's degree in Deaf Education from McDaniel College. Amy co-authored a book with her mother, *Amy Signs: A Mother and Her Deaf Daughter*, and their Stories in 2012. She lives with her four beloved cats, three of whom are deaf.

Robert Chadwick grew up in Auburn, Nebraska, and lived in Omaha and Lincoln before settling down in Columbus, Nebraska. Photographing rock concerts has been Robert's side-profession for the last five years. He also does portrait and family photography. Robert's day job is as a Structural Civil Drafter at Nebraska Public Power District where he has worked for 31 years. His wife Kellie McDermott-Chadwick is originally from Florida, and they have a high-energy three year old cat, Keanu. You can see Robert's unique photos and hire him for any special photographic projects by checking out his Facebook page https://www.facebook.com/robertchadwickphotography/. Follow him on Instagram at @ rachadw66 or his online concert magazine at @govenue.

Chris Grassmeyer has four grown sons, the youngest of whom is deaf. She loves spending time with family and taking road trips. Someday she hopes to retire in Florida. Chris is a proud dog mom to two Yorkipoos.

Max Grassmeyer grew up in Fremont, Nebraska and commuted to Omaha daily to attend school there. He and his wife live in Omaha, Nebraska and have three cats. Photo credit: Kendall Grassmeyer.

CPSIA information can be obtained
at www.ICGtesting.com
Printed in the USA
LVHW071925160220
647112LV00002B/8